Milly Bean, Jungle Queen

Written by Martin Waddell

Illustrated by Ana Martín Larrañaga

WALKER BOOKS
AND SUBSIDIARIES
LONDON • BOSTON • SYDNEY

"Don't go in the jungle,"
the birds told Milly Bean.
"You'll get eaten!"

"I'm not scared of nuffink!"
said Milly.

Into the jungle went Milly.
She sssssssss-ed at a snake
and tied him in knots.
That was the end of
the snake.

She bashed a baboon
with a banana.
That was the end of
the baboon.

She booed at a bear
and made faces.
That was the end of
the bear.

"I am Milly Bean,
Queen of the Jungle!"
she boasted.
"I am Queen Milly,
and this is my throne!"
And Milly sat down
on her throne.

Of *course* it was
AN ALLIGATOR.

The alligator ate her.
And that was the end
of Milly Bean!

To my sister Usua
A.M.L.

First published 2001 by Walker Books Ltd
87 Vauxhall Walk, London SE11 5HJ

4 6 8 10 9 7 5 3

Text © 2001 Martin Waddell
Illustrations © 2001 Ana Martín Larrañaga

The right of Martin Waddell to be identified as author of this work has been asserted
by him in accordance with the Copyright, Designs and Patents Act 1988

This book has been typeset in Avant Garde

Printed in Hong Kong

British Library Cataloguing in Publication Data:
a catalogue record for this book
is available from the British Library

ISBN 0-7445-8303-9